Happy Grouchy Day

by Suzanne Weyn   illustrated by John Lund

Featuring Jim Henson's Sesame Street Muppets

Random House 🏠 New York

Copyright © 1999 Children's Television Workshop (CTW). Sesame Street Muppets © 1999 The Jim Henson Company. All rights reserved under International and Pan-American Copyright Conventions. Published in the United States by Random House, Inc., New York, and simultaneously in Canada by Random House of Canada Limited, Toronto, in conjunction with Children's Television Workshop. Sesame Street, the Sesame Street sign, and CTW Books are trademarks and service marks of Children's Television Workshop.
Library of Congress Cataloging-in-Publication Data
Weyn, Suzanne.
Happy grouchy day / by Suzanne Weyn ; illustrated by John Lund. — p.   cm. — (The adventures of Elmo in Grouchland)
"Featuring Jim Henson's Sesame Street Muppets." Summary: Oscar tries to explain to Grizzy that she should be rude and messy and rotten because she lives in Grouchland.
ISBN 0-375-80133-2
[1. Behavior—Fiction. 2. Puppets—Fiction.]
I. Lund, John (John H.), ill. II. Title. III. Series. PZ7.W539Hap 1999 [E]—dc21 98-43776
Printed in the United States of America 10 9 8 7 6 5 4 3 2 1
www.randomhouse.com/kids
www.sesamestreet.com

Welcome to Grouchland! It's icky! It's yucchy! It's smelly!
Just the way we Grouches like it.

"Pee-yew!" said Elmo. "Well, at least it's a beautiful day.
The sun is shining. The sky is blue. The birds are singing."

"Blech," said Oscar. "A nice damp drizzle would be much better."

"Listen!" said Elmo. "What is that noise?"
"Where?" said Oscar. He listened.
"It sounds like crying," Oscar said finally.

"Is it the tree?" said Oscar.

"Oh, that's not a tree crying. It's a little Grouch!" said Elmo.

"Grizzy!" Oscar said. "What are you doing here?"

"Why are you sad?" Elmo asked.

"I got into trouble in school today," Grizzy explained. "The teacher called my parents. My mom and dad will be *so* angry at me."

"What did you do?" asked Elmo.

"It was an awful day!" said Grizzy.
"My friend's block tower fell, so I helped her build a new one."

"My teacher was carrying lots of books, and I held the door open for him."

"I cleaned up after myself at lunchtime."

"You're a very nice girl," said Elmo. "But Elmo doesn't understand why you're crying."

"You don't?" Oscar yelled. "She was a terrible, terrible Grouch. In Grouchland you are supposed to be *unhelpful, rude,* and *messy.* That's the Grouchland way. Now here's what you should have done..."

"You should have laughed when that kid's blocks fell."

"*Never* open the door for anyone."

"And *never, ever* throw away trash. Trash is what we Grouches love most of all!"

"No!" gasped Elmo.

"Yes," said Oscar. "That is the grouchy way. Trust me. It's what all little Grouches have to learn."

"I don't know how to do that," said Grizzy sadly. "I'm just a misfit."

"Naah," said Oscar. "You're just not trying. Here, watch me." He ran up to a Grouch mom and her baby. "That's a really scrappy-looking kid!" he yelled.

"Thanks. Have a grouchy day," said the mom, smiling.

"Here comes another baby," Oscar said to Grizzy. "You try it."
Grizzy rushed to the stroller. "What a...what a..."

"What a *cute* baby!" Grizzy cried.

"The nerve!" snapped the angry Grouch mom. "Go away, little girl. And learn some Grouch manners!"

"She's hopeless," Oscar sighed.

Oscar and Elmo walked Grizzy home through the park. Along the way, Grizzy saw a cat stuck in a tree. "Let me help you, kitty cat," said Grizzy.

"Grizzy!" Oscar called.

Grizzy forced herself to be grouchy. "Forget it, cat," she shouted. "Are you crazy? I'm not helping you. You got yourself up there. Get yourself down!"

"You did it!" said Oscar. "Way to go!"

"I did it! I did it!" Grizzy shouted happily. "I was really, really grouchy!"

"Watch this!" Grizzy shouted. She ran up to some old Grouch ladies. She stuck her tongue out at them. She blew a great big razzberry at them. "Neener, neener, neener!"

"What a lovely child," said one of the ladies.

"So rude and grouchy," said another.

Grizzy bounced up and down with delight. "I've got it! I'm a real Grouch. This is the happiest, grouchiest day of my life. Thank you, Oscar."

"Hey, kid, watch it with the 'thank you' business," Oscar said with a scowl.

"Oops! I almost forgot," Grizzy said. Then she stuck her tongue out at him.

"Nah, nah, nah-nah, nah," she said.

"Now that's the way to end a perfect grouchy day," said Oscar.

"If you say so," said Elmo. "But when you come to Sesame Street, please have a *nice* day."